That Dog!

Level 2C

Written by Sam Hay
Illustrated by Vian Oelofsen
Reading Consultant: Betty Franchi

About Phonics

Spoken English uses more than 40 speech sounds. Each sound is called a *phoneme*. Some phonemes relate to a single letter (d-o-g) and others to combinations of letters (sh-ar-p). When a phoneme is written down, it is called a *grapheme*. Teaching these sounds, matching them to their written form, and sounding out words for reading is the basis of phonics.

Early phonics instruction gives children the tools to sound out, blend, and say the words without having to rely on memory or guesswork. This instruction gives children the confidence and ability to read unfamiliar words, helping them progress toward independent reading.

About the Consultant

Betty Franchi is an American educator with
a Bachelor's Degree in Elementary and Middle
Education as well as a Master's Degree in Special
Education. Betty holds a National Boards for
Professional Teaching Standards certification.
Throughout her 24 years as a teacher, she has
studied and developed an expertise in Phonetic
Awareness and has implemented phonetic strategies,
teaching many young children to read, including
students with special needs.

Reading tips

 This book focuses on the *th* sound.

Tricky and/or new words in this book

Any words in bold may have unusual spellings
or are new and have not yet been introduced.

Tricky and/or new words in this book

**the   my   are   to   friend
was   said   they   good**

Extra ways to have fun with this book

After the readers have finished the story, ask them
questions about what they have just read.

Who rescues Tim and Ken?
What mischief does Chip get into?

Make flashcards for each of the sounds within the
pronunciation guide. This will help reinforce letter/
sound matches.

I like to read quietly
in my bed. Sometimes
I read to myself, but mostly
I read out loud.

A Pronunciation Guide

This grid highlights the sounds used in the story and offers a guide on how to say them.

s as in sat	a as in ant	t as in tin	p as in pig	i as in ink
n as in net	c as in cat	e as in egg	h as in hen	r as in rat
m as in mug	d as in dog	g as in get	o as in ox	u as in up
l as in log	f as in fan	b as in bag	j as in jug	v as in van
w as in wet	z as in zip	y as in yet	k as in kit	qu as in quick
x as in box	ff as in off	ll as in ball	ss as in kiss	zz as in buzz
ck as in duck	pp as in puppy	nn as in bunny	rr as in arrow	gg as in egg
dd as in daddy	bb as in chubby	tt as in attic	sh as in shop	ch as in chip
th as in them				

Be careful not to add an /uh/ sound to /s/, /t/, /p/, /c/, /h/, /r/, /m/, /d/, /g/, /l/, /f/ and /b/. For example, say /ff/ not /fuh/ and /sss/ not /suh/.

Dad is mad. "That dog got mud on **the** rug!" Mom is fed up. "That dog sat on **my** hat!"

Tim is sad.
"Chip is not a bad dog!"

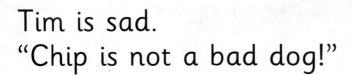

Dad and Tim **are** in the van.
Tim is off **to** camp.

Chip will miss Tim.

Dad and Tim got a shock at
the camp. Chip **was** in the van.

"This is not a dog camp!" **said** Dad.
"Sit in the van, bad dog!"

Tim spots his best **friend** Ken.

They run up a hill.

But at the top they get lost.

"Dad! Help!" yells Tim.

"Tim?" said Dad.
But Dad cannot see them.

Then Chip runs up the hill.

Chip sees them!

Tim got a big lick!

"That dog is **good**!" said Dad.

But then Chip spots a pond.
Plop! Chip is in the pond.

Then Chip runs back to them. "Yuck!" said Dad. "That is a bad smell. But Chip is a good dog."

OVER **48** TITLES IN SIX LEVELS
Betty Franchi recommends...

Some titles from Level 1

I love reading phonics — **Bad Rat**
978 1 84898 747 0

I love reading phonics — **The Best Gift**
978 1 84898 750 0

I love reading phonics — **Clint and Grant Play I-Spy**
978 1 84898 752 4

I love reading phonics — **Bret and Grandma's Trip!**
978 1 84898 751 7

Other titles to enjoy from Level 2

I love reading phonics — **Chuck and Duck**
978 1 84898 756 2

I love reading phonics — **Let's go to the Swings**
978 1 84898 759 3

I love reading phonics — **Kyle in Trouble**
978 1 84898 762 3

Some titles from Level 3

I love reading phonics — **Bart's Go-Cart**
978 1 84898 768 5

I love reading phonics — **Queen Ella's Feet**
978 1 84898 764 7

I love reading phonics — **Puff Flies**
978 1 84898 765 4

I love reading phonics — **The Pop Duet**
978 1 84898 767 8

An Hachette Company
First Published in the United States by TickTock, an imprint of Octopus Publishing Group.
www.octopusbooksusa.com

Copyright © Octopus Publishing Group Ltd 2013

Distributed in the US by
Hachette Book Group USA
237 Park Avenue, New York NY 10017, USA

Distributed in Canada by
Canadian Manda Group
165 Dufferin Street, Toronto, Ontario, Canada M6K 3H6

ISBN 978 1 84898 757 9

Printed and bound in China
10 9 8 7 6 5 4 3 2 1